HERE'S SOMETHING ABOUT SAM

By HANNAH BARNABY

Pictures by ANNE WILSDORF

HOUGHTON MIFFLIN HARCOURT
BOSTON NEW YORK

For James—a whole wide
world of friends awaits you —H.B.

For my favorite little monsters:
Hector and Virgile —A.W.

hmhbooks.com

The illustrations in this book were done in watercolor and ink.
The text type was set in Aunt Mildred.
The display type was hand-lettered by Anne Wilsdorf.

Designed by Natalie Fondriest

Library of Congress Cataloging-in-Publication Data is on file.

ISBN: 978-1-328-76680-9

Manufactured in China
SCP 10 9 8 7 6 5 4 3 2 1
4500794986

Max was having a sleepover for his birthday.
He made invitations for all the boys in his class.
Well, almost all the boys.

"What about Michael?" his mother asked. "And isn't there a new boy? What's his name?"

"Michael picks his nose," said Max. "And the new kid is Sam. There's something different about him."

"What do you mean?" asked his mother.

"I don't know," said Max. "Just ... something."

"Well," said Max's mother, "that's no reason to leave him out. I'm sure you'll like him when you get to know him better."

Max suspected that his mother had never been a third-grader. But he made two more cards.

The next day at school, he handed out the invitations. All the boys said they would come. Well, almost all the boys.

"I'm not sure I can," Sam said.
"There's a full moon that night."

"There's something about that kid," Max told Michael at lunch.

"Sam is cool," Michael said. "He can run really fast."

"I don't know what it is," Max told Elliott at recess.

"Sam is awesome," said Elliott. "He always knows what's cooking in the cafeteria way before lunchtime."

But Max was sure he was right.
And by the time Sam said he
could come to the sleepover, Max
was determined to figure it out.

First they had dinner.

"I like my hamburgers rare," Sam told Max's father.

"Gross," said Michael. But Max thought the way the red juice ran down Sam's chin was mesmerizing.

Then they played Twister.

"Hey!" Jeremy yelled. "Sam tried to bite me!"

"Weird," said Elliott. But Max couldn't help smiling just a little.

They put on their pajamas to watch *Night of the Zombie Squirrels.*

"I'm going to change in the bathroom," said Sam.

"Why?" asked Jeremy.

But Sam came back wearing the BIONIC BAT pajamas that Max had wanted forever.

"Cookies!" Max's mother
sang when she came in.
Michael grabbed a cookie.
Elliott grabbed a cookie.
Jeremy grabbed
two cookies.

When Max reached for a cookie,
his hand bumped into Sam's.
Sam's hand was covered with hair.
His claws were long and sharp.

All the boys shrieked and hid in their
sleeping bags. Well, almost all the boys.
"Cool!" said Max.

Sam pulled his hand back
and tucked it into his pocket.
"There's—um—something
you should know about me."
Just then the room was
flooded with moonlight.

Sam growled and ran out to the backyard.
"Awesome!" said Max.

Sam and Max stayed up all night.

Elliott, Michael, and Jeremy did too.

Well, almost all night.

The next day, after everyone had
gone home, Max's mother said,
"That Sam is an unusual boy."
"Yep," Max said, "he sure
is something."